Prologue

This is my first book; just some amateur writing to taste the waters and mostly to make sense of my thoughts; here's to hoping that you will like reading this book.

The reader should not get bored, keeping in mind this, I have tried to write it in a lucid way and at the same time have also tried not to deviate from the content. I have tried every possible way to avoid distracting the reader from the Centre plot of the story.

Deepak, a gentleman from India, falls prey to a girl's dark intentions and this story takes you through his journey of grilling romance, suspense and thriller page by page...

GIRL WITH THE TWISTED TATTOO

KANHAIYA K

Copyright © Kanhaiya K
All Rights Reserved.

This book has been published with all efforts taken to make the material error-free after the consent of the author. However, the author and the publisher do not assume and hereby disclaim any liability to any party for any loss, damage, or disruption caused by errors or omissions, whether such errors or omissions result from negligence, accident, or any other cause.

While every effort has been made to avoid any mistake or omission, this publication is being sold on the condition and understanding that neither the author nor the publishers or printers would be liable in any manner to any person by reason of any mistake or omission in this publication or for any action taken or omitted to be taken or advice rendered or accepted on the basis of this work. For any defect in printing or binding the publishers will be liable only to replace the defective copy by another copy of this work then available.

Contents

Prologue

This is my first book; just some amateur writing to taste the waters and mostly to make sense of my thoughts; here's to hoping that you will like reading this book.

The reader should not get bored, keeping in mind this, I have tried to write it in a lucid way and at the same time have also tried not to deviate from the content. I have tried every possible way to avoid distracting the reader from the Centre plot of the story.

Deepak, a gentleman from India, falls prey to a girl's dark intentions and this story takes you through his journey of grilling romance, suspense and thriller page by page...

ONE
THE MEETING

Having just landed at J F Kennedy international airport, New York City - the city of dreams for many people across the globe, whether it is for study, work or tourism, Deepak, who was no different than million other pursuant of the land of the dreams coming in the Big Apple, walked up to the immigration window, passport in one hand, eyes full of hope but rounded by amazement.

The job that landed him in this city was of an associate at a top investment banking firm.

The young lady at the immigration desk asked for his visa, Deepak, who was staring at her, came to his senses and handed his passport to the lady officer, who had a twisted tattoo on right side of her neck. She also noticed Deepak staring her neck and just smiled clearing Deepak's arrival in NYC.

~

It was a Sunday morning of August. Deepak stood on the balcony of his company-provided 1 BHK studio apartment at the famous Troika Living, enjoying the sunshine of the city of New York. While looking around, something just front of his balcony, about a distance of some 50 meter, caught his eyes. A young lady with the same dragon tattoo on right side of her neck was sitting in her balcony with her face away from him, engrossed in a zine; in first glimpse she seemed like the girl whom he met at the airport, and all of a sudden his mind zoned out of his senses, imagining the beauty, and drifting in scenarios of what could have been.

A sudden movement brought his attention back to the balcony - the girl was waving at him! At first he did not seem to realize that it was him she was waving at, but then he looked around and saw no one else so, he strained his eyes a little more and could not believe at what he was looking at - it was her! So, his hand automatically went up in the air, waving side to side, nervously albeit.

His heart started racing, pulse were rushing; not in his wildest dreams could he have imagined meeting her like this again so, with this big push of fate he decided that he would not hold back from pursuing her.

"Hey, Shelly, wassup!"

"Hi Deepak! Crazy seeing you here, right? What are the chances!.. I hope you're not stalking me (laughs)"

Deepak just grinned like a starstruck mime.

"So, is this your apartment or are you visiting a friend?"

"..eh, yes! no, it's mine."

"So, it's Sunday - how's it going so far. Any plans for the evening?"

"Nothing much really. Don't know anyone yet, but I am going out for a movie tonight."

"Which one?"

"You know, the new Spiderman."

"Sounds interesting.. look, I don't want to impose or anything but if you want I can come with."

Now this was an offer no guy in his right mine would refuse so the obvious answer Deepak went for was a "sure, why not!".

"What time should I pick you at?"

"7. We'll grab a drink at Tim's Bar before hitting the theatre; hope you won't mind."

"Not at all, see you at 7 then!"

"See ya!"

Now, you are thinking of who's this Shelly? Came, all of sudden in the middle. So clearing your curiosity, she was the same young lady whom Deepak wanted to talk. Now you'll think how this did happen. So Next...............

On that Sunday Morning, when Deepak saw the lady from his balcony, he decided to see her daily from the comfort of his balcony. So, the plan gone well, Deepak waited patiently in the wake of her notice. His patience paid and She noticed it that this boy sat daily in his balcony without failing a single day. He also noticed it that she was noticing him now. This juggernaut goes ahead patiently and one evening he tracked her down to nearby eateries ordering pizza.

Thus, both went to the movie night, where besides Deepak and Shelly some of the Deepak's Colleague was also there enjoying the evening.

Thus begins the journey that lead to the fate of our protagonist's plan most of which would unfold in coming pages.

TWO

THE
PERTURBATION

Jack called Deepak to discuss some new business coming in India. Jack presented the matter before Deepak to get his take on that. The matter was that one of the big tourist companies in Goa had been under severe stress as Co-vid hit the nation. Tourism sectors were the most hit sectors in the world and India as well. The Company has 20 million dollar loan and was mounting its interest over the principle. So, the scenario was clear to take up the case and resolve the issue. Deepak nodded in yes to question of Jack to work upon. Jack was as an Indian, eager to work on this case, at least Indian better know the Indian market sentiments and data.

Deepak came straight to his cubical to ponder over the issue, how it would settle the case and started studying the financial data received from Jack, the VP of the group. Deepak was as happy as Jack as it was his first major case over there to work upon as associate to the group. So, he started experimenting his financial modeling skills and making the charts to reach a solution between the parties.

His mind contemplating on many issue related to work except work one more thing is hovering in his mind that is Shelly. Her beauty was so attractive to Deepak was that his thought was impending his work. He tried hard to concentrate but the heart inside compelling him to think over her. What was that her eye, her lips or just her tattoo at her neck.

It's already past midnight working on the model chart and it seems he was committed to the work that night only. But finally he decided to sleep as it was 2 a.m. in the morning. Work stopped and this is the instance, he can fully devote his thought to her.

He got up and run to balcony with grudging eye as ray of sun like tyndall effect coming from the window panes with curtain aside but he was late today. It was already 8 in the morning and she left for the work. Deepak felt very sad and drowsy in that morning as if his something important missed. Obviously it was important for him who had not had a taste of attraction of any girl in India. It is the first instance when a girl gave him attention.

Jack called Deepak to discuss over Goa tourism company stress debt and Deepak came with his mammoth work done by him over the night playing with financial data and models. Deepak stresses the issue on selling the debt with some big corporate who can bear its debt. The company's reputation was not bad, if it sustained, it would be good decision by some big corporate who could bear this stress for a short period of time. Jack nodded in agreement and decided to visit Goa.

The next Sunday, they arrived at Goa and stayed at hotel Marriott. Next day they are required to visit the office of that distressed company. Mr. Fernandez welcomed both the men came from the other continent to ward off his company from the distress. Deepak presented his models of financial data to him, how will they provide solution to their crises. Deepak asked them to sell off its debt laden company with some stable and high income corporate who can bear its current jolt and get return from the same once the situation of pandemic got over. Listening patiently, Mr Fernandez agreed with Deepak's view.

Jack wanted to take a tour of Goa and some important places in India like the Taj Mahal, Delhi's Heritage sites etc but Deepak who was just fallen in love with that immigration officer wanted to move to New York with the first available flight. Again he was in a fix whether he should convince Jack to return immediately or should stay with him for India tour.

Deepak was really in a fix over the issue that was going on in his conscience but he had to choose stay or go. Eventually he chose to stay in India for tour with his boss Jack. They first went to see the Taj on Tuesday and spent all that day at Taj only. Even Deepak hadn't seen the Taj earlier, though he was residing in India. Deepak, however know a little bit of Taj from school textbook or general public consensus. He shared that little bit knowledge with Jack, so that jack could not believe that he hadn't seen the beautiful Taj even though residing in India. The day ends with dinner at a local cuisine restaurant though it was good enough to attract foreigners like US.

Next day was at Delhi, everyone knows about it, being the National capital and thanks to textbook, which covers its history in very lucid manner. So, both went 1st to red fort, then India gate, Qu tub minar and so on enjoying the full day at Delhi's Heritage sites and beauty both of them stayed at hotel oberoi in Delhi. Deepak was happy as his India tour is culminating for this time. He was too eager to catch 1st

available flight in the next morning as if someone special is waiting for him. Whether it is or not from her end but in his mind shelly is special.

Deepak boarded the 1st flight to New York next morning from IGI airport Delhi. In the nonstop 15 hrs flight he hardly slept an hour. Thinking of that girl who's controlling Deepak's nerve these days. Announcement made we are reaching to New York shortly, passengers are requested to fasten the seat belt please. An elated face of Deepak's fasten the same as soon as announcement made and as scheduled, the plane landed at the air strip. Suddenly Deepak's thought went to his 1st landing at this airport, when he met with that tattoo girl. It seemed that the same scene was being repeated but that time Deepak was frank and naive to the city and everyone over there but this time neither was he naive for the city nor for anyone. This time he was known to someone and city as well.

THREE
THE REUNION

Crossing the emigration desk, his eye looking for only one eye in the crowd but to no avail. She was not available at the desk and not finding her, he was somehow felt sad and thought that her shift may be changed. Clearing all formalities at the airport he directly went to his apartment before biding adieu to Jack in another taxi.

Taking rest for few hours as he barely slept in flight though it was business class, for which his company borne the cost. Taking coffee in one hand Deepak stands waited for her to come at her balcony but to no avail.

It was 6th day for Deepak without looking her. In these six day hardly a minute Deepak didn't thought of her. But physically she was still at distance from him although he was just near her. So, Deepak decided to knock the door of her while taking evening walk. He felt that would be a good idea and eventually it works.

It was 8 in the evening, when Deepak knocked at the door of shelly. No response! Deepak again knocked the door and door opened and the beautiful was in front of him. His face just elated with joy from the inside. Deepak entered the house and sat at the sofa nearby as directed by shelly.

Shelly: - Tea or coffee?

Deepak: - Coffee!

Shelly went to kitchen for preparing coffee for him and herself. Deepak was just wondering and trying to get some words so that they can talk.

Shelly: - Your coffee!

Deepak: - Thank you!

It was a pin drop silence!

Then, shelly started asking Deepak regarding their Job and India tour. Deepak also wanted something to talk, so shelly solved his problem.

Deepak narrated all his India business trip and other stuff that they did during the trip. Deepak also mentioned the Taj Mahal and its beauty.

Deepak: - You are not at the airport today?

Shelly:- Yeh! today I was on leave.

Deepak:- All well?

Shelly:- yeh! I am fine. Just wanted !

Deepak:- Oh!

Shelly:- When did you come?

Deepak:- From the same flight, when we first see each other.

Shelly:- Good to see you again.

Deepak:- Here too!

Deepak:- didn't saw you at the airport, so, I decided to check whether are you ok?

Shelly:- Thank you!

Deepak stood up to go and said bye. But shelly did not want him to go tonight. So shelly asked him to stay there for tonight. Deepak nodded in agreement.

They went to nearby eateries for dinner, where Deepak ordered American crispy chicken slices and chicken pizza and red wine for her and same dishes but whisky for himself. Cheering each other and enjoying dinner. Deepak was so excited today as it's his first dinner date. Shelly was also excited but not as much as Deepak.

Shelly's gave the key to Deepak to open the door. As soon as Deepak opened door, Shelly forces herself on him. Started kissing, Deepak was nervous and reluctant as he was not able to sense the happening, it was so fast and intense that he cannot resist himself for longer against the will of that girl. So, initially resisting her, Deepak falls prey to her and started giving response as intensely as her. They have reached to sofa in the living room still not left kissing to each other. Now Deepak took the charge and force himself upon her over the sofa. After kissing episode both of them took a break but it was not over that night. Deepak went to the bar area and took out a bottle of whisky. Now both were too high to control themselves. Sitting beside each other both were looking straight into each-other's eye full of lust. They bend towards each other and started kissing lips of each other. After kissing ten minutes, Deepak lifted shelly and went to the bedroom, where all the night they made intense love.

FOUR

THE BREAKER

Next morning Deepak went to office with elated face. Sitting at cafeteria, thinking of last night adventure he had done, that was completely beyond the extent of his nature.

Jack came to him wishing him good morning, he responds coming to his senses, as he was engaged with his thought. Jack asked him what he had been thinking sensing his discomfort while he wished him. Deepak replied with shyness nothing! Being American Jack didn't dig upon him as in his culture no-one interested in others personal interest till you allowed.

Jack went to his office having coffee with Deepak. Deepak also followed the same path. Deepak went to Jack's office with his financial models that he worked upon to close the Goa resort deal and it was to sell the company at valuing 30 million dollars to some big corporate, so that the existing company could get some extra money and his bank as well. Eventually one Chinese company interested in the deal, seeing growing tourist inflow to India since the current Govt took charge. Jack asked him to fix a meeting with the Chinese company which showed interest with him and the Goan Company at the Goa resort. Deepak nodded and asked the secretary to coordinate accordingly.

It was 8 in the evening, Deepak still in the office engulfed in his work. Secretary saw it and asked him what is so important to work late in evening, almost everyone has been gone. Deepak nodded and said not so important just working and forgot the time, just going said the Deepak.

Deepak came to home at 9 PM and suddenly he remembered that he hasn't talk to shelly today even once. This is the first time Deepak even didn't thought of her. So, immediately he called Shelly but for no avail. He again called but no response. He thought she may be somewhere else and phone is on silent or may be at work. Deepak went to sleep as he feels tired today being exhaustive work at office.

It was 6 in the morning Deepak standing at his balcony with coffee mug in his hand as usual waiting for a glimpse of her first love, as time passes but she didn't appear. So he called her again but no response from other side. He tried twice but no response. So he decided to go to meet her physically. As soon as he proceeds towards her apartment he got call from his boss to come to office earlier as something important to discuss with him. He stopped going towards her apartment rather came back and started dressing himself for office.

He went office rather to meet her. As soon as he entered the office, secretary tells him that Jack wanted to meet him. He nodded and went to Jack cabin.

"What's the matter Jack" said Deepak.

Jack asked him to sit and started praising his due diligence over the couple of months since joining.

But Deepak again under vague thought what prompted Jack to call him office earlier. So Deepak again asked what the matter was that you needed to call me office earlier.

Breaking the ice, Jack congratulated him and told about his promotion as VP from the associate. Deepak elated listening all this. But something also Jack has in his basket to told him that would be not good for Deepak and what's that. That was his transfer from New York to London.

As soon as Jack communicated him about this development, Deepak shocked. Jack can clearly perceive it from his appearance. So Jack asked whether there were any problem. Deepak nodded in negative. So what's bothering you as it seems from your look. You should be happy as promotion in such a short period is not regular here. It takes at least a year or another to become VP from an associate. But you got it just within 8 months of work i.e. management is valuing your contribution to the organization. Deepak nodded in agreement.

Jack again congratulating him and told that the arrangement of transfer will take a week's time. You will be working here till then.

So with low feeling, Deepak came to his apartment, consoling himself for the fate and grieving as well. He then called shelly but no response. He tried it again, the same result. It was frustrating experience for the Deepak. He tried and went Shelley's apartment why she was not picking up the call. He knocked but gate not opened. He knocked but the same response. He again tried calling her. Again she was not responding.

He came back to his apartment with heavy heart, ate some bread left in fridge and went to sleep. Thinking of shelly, why she was not picking up his phone, why she wasn't at home. This was not the time of her work. All this thought hovering in his mind throughout the night.

In the morning, he, as usual waiting for her appearance at balcony, thinking of her and his transfer to London. Both the development is saddening for him. If he goes to London then he hardly see her, which was his first love. He obviously didn't want to lose her. So he thought, will request Jack to do something to stop his transfer. But where was Shelly, it's been 36 hrs to talk or see with her. Whether something wrong happened to her, now this thought stroked his mind. What could happen, now her phone is even not reachable?

He went to office next morning some earlier than his usual time, as he was feeling sad at home, thought of Shelly not left him for a single minute. So he came to office earlier. As soon as he entered his office, secretary came and congratulate for his promotion. Deepak thanked him with little or even fake smile. Julia, picked his smile and asked why he was feeling sad. Deepak denied and said no! I am happy, but Julia insist, then Deepak said all the things he was going through in his mind. Julia consoled him or what else could she do? He merely worked that day, feeling low throughout the day. As soon as office hour ends he rushed to her work place, asking about her with her colleagues. Everyone gave the same reply that no one saw her since two days. Neither had she applied for leave. Her office colleagues were as worrisome as him, but it's been two days still no one reported it to police. So one of her colleague and he decided to go to police and reported her missing report. It's now almost clear that something bad would happen with her. Deepak's heart was grieving tremendously and no-one over there to console him.

It's now more difficult for Deepak to leave New York without knowing the truth what could happen to Shelly. Why she was missing. Now police was working on the missing complaint. They were enquiring at hospitals and control room for any incidents to check with that.

In-between, Deepak decided to ask Jack for stopping his transfer if possible, so the next day he informally asked Jack if there were any possibilities of staying his transfer to London. Jack told him may be. He'd try to convince the management if he could. Deepak somehow relaxed with the tone of Jack, that seemed work would be done in his favor.

Deepak came to his cuboidal and thought of the Police and called the Police station enquiring about the progress of the case. They told him very firmly that they were working and in this they were enquiring about any incidents and matching it with control room and hospitals. Also they informed all the police stations and mobile vans with their photo to see any development. If anything found they would communicate. Deepak felt that police was working with due diligence in the case and hoping case would be detected.

FIVE

THE SHOCKER

Days passed but no information of the Shelly reported. It'd been 5 days but no call from police. He decided to visit the police station with the same colleague of Shelly. So he went to Shelly's work place to see her colleague and asked her to accompany him to the Police station. She agreed and accompanied him. Both went to the Police and asked officer In Charge about the case. The OIC told them very politely the development on the case. Unfortunately they hadn't found her in any of the incidents in the city as confirmed by the control room and hospitals. He didn't forget to say that she might be deliberately missed, but his hunt was on if anything could found cognizable then he would communicate to them.

Both Deepak and Myra exited the police station with heavy heart and discussing about the Shelly. Why did she hide themselves deliberately? Was there any issues with her personal life? Both agreed and confirmed each other in negative for any such possibilities. Now one angle was only something bad happened with her. Either she had been kidnapped or something else like any criminal activities. So, it will be cleared only if case was solved.

Deepak came to his home dropping Myra at her apartment near Hudson river. Since the missing of Shelly, Deepak's life becoming hell of hopelessness as it's the 1st time someone loved him. Deepak decided to apply his mind in discovering the truth behind the missing. So he simultaneously started his investigation too apart from the Police. Now he started closely recounting all the event happened with her, when they are together, from his first visit from airport to last at her apartment.

He wanted to leave no stone unturned in unearthing the truth. So in this line he took 15 days leave from the office and 2nd most important work he needed to do was to convince Myra to accompany him in this investigation, as Myra was local and had spent time with Shelly. He called Myra to meet in the evening at the restro near her office. Myra agreed but confused, why Deepak wanted to meet her as they met just last evening and met the police also. Deepak didn't clear anything on phone to her. Before meeting her in evening, Deepak had done his homework jotting all the things down at paper so that he could convince Myra.

Hi! Myra

Hi! Deepak

As expected, Myra asked him, why he called her today there. Deepak explained all the things to her what he had worked upon. Myra sipping her coffee listened all the things very calmly. But Myra didn't agree with him as it could be dangerous to intervene in the work of police. Deepak tried to convince her that they will not interfere with police work but can work in parallel. Deepak was stubborn that police was not doing his work properly and so they needed to work themselves.

He went to the apartment where she lived and broke into her house. He searched every nook and corner with chary eyes. He looked to kitchen where everything was as it was, as was that day when he stayed there. He got nothing useful there he went to cupboard and searched everything but no avail. As he was leaving her house his mind stuck at locker that was left open. He run through the same and watch it with caution but nothing was available in the locker except some paper, that were also not clear for what was it. It seemed to be some map of Delhi and New York.

Then he came to his house and called Myra regarding her apartment and conveyed that nothing credible was found over there. Myra consoled him and said will get something at office. He also tried to convince her that he could get at office but she refused as it was too risky and said she would get through all the stuff lying with her at her workstation or office. It was 7th day since the missing of Shelly. Deepak trying to console himself and left for the route, which was followed by her while going home to office. They took a taxi and asked taxi driver to go at slow pace, he would compensate his loss for the time taken. Driver nodded in agreement and started the journey. It was weird for the driver as Taxi driver tried to convince himself which kind of this guy is, people asked driver to go fast generally but this one is just opposite.

Travelling through the route Deepak observing and noticing every nook and corner where it could be possible or danger to life and he found a dark place where anyone can be kidnapped. He asked driver to stop and left taxi paying his fare. Then he wandered there poking his nose here and there. It was a place of godowns and seems old industrial complex that was now defunct. Going through one of the street he heard some noise. He stopped and decided to learn what the noise were. He went to the shutter and sneaked with a tiny hole present in it and what he saw was unexpected and shocking as well. He shocked and felt he wasn't seeing it. He picked his skin to believe it now he realized that it's real. He saw Shelly surrounded by some 4 armed men and even Shelly was armed. They were discussing some attack in India, but what kind of attack it was, he not listened properly. Now he was too curious to listen so he tried to listen it very cautiously. Now what he was listening were beyond his expectations and tried not to believe it with his own ear. Listening their talk he returned with heavy heart and unconvincing now his love turned into hate for Shelly. But still he was thinking what he saw and listened may not be the correct but it was. So, he went straight to his apartment and took a warm bath to relax himself.

How could he relax after seeing Shelly's reality? Now another scenario came in front of him. Earlier he was anxious with her missing and now he was even more anxious seeing her with non-state actors.

Next morning, he again took a cup of coffee and went to stand at that Balcony but today his mood was not the same like other day. It seems he was never met her. He proceeds all the daily work as usual and felt relaxed. He went office even without completing his leave. He sat in his cuboidal and working as if nothing was happened with him.

Julia saw him and went to her greeting good morning. In return Deepak said very good morning.

Julia: - You came early.

Deepak: - What do you mean?

Julia: - I meant that still your leave was balance and you are here.

Deepak: - okkie! Work completed earlier than expected, so I came back. Once planned work were completed what could I do in this new City.

Julia: - Yeh. That's right.

Then Julia asked about Shelly. Deepak said, that was past. Julia understood he is not in mood to talk about her. So she came back to her seat.

Jack called, Deepak seeing him in cuboidal. Jack asked, what happened you didn't complete your leave. Deepak nodded and reluctantly replied yeh! Jack didn't ask anything about leave sensing Deepak's reluctance.

So, what's doing today, Jack asked Deepak.

Just reviewing financial model made for Goan Company, Deepak said.

No need now for that, we have managed that work. We got that Chinese company, which you suggested for take over on board and got signed the contract. They liked your work and thesis on the project and concluded to do the business with Goan company. Thanks, you became a in demand business associate in a short time here in the company.

After experiencing all this, now Deepak didn't want to live in this city and hence urge for his transfer to Jack.

Jack Surprised and asked are you ok!

Deepak said yeh! very firmly.

Jack said, earlier you have declined the offer and so I have also communicated your decision for further process.

Deepak asked for any option left! very sadly!

Jack replied and told to wait!

Next Morning, Jack met with Deepak with smiling face at the cafeteria of the office as usual sipping coffee over there. Ending his conversation, Jack asked Deepak to meet him at office, some god news is was waiting for him. Deepak nodded with elated face.

Deepak entered Jack's cabin and asked for the good news!

Jack handed him his transfer order to London and asked are you sure! Deepak Nodded! Ok then your joining to London office is within a week. Good Luck!